This book unfortunately belongs to:

Cooper

This book is dedicated to anyone who likes candy corn.

The most misunderstood corn of all...

www.ackersbooks.com

Entire World Books: 7

Melanie was too busy drinking a Pumpkin Spice Latte to help.

ISBN-13: 978-1-951046-13-2

The WORST HALLOWEEN Book

in the Whole Entire World

Joey Acker

Trick or treat...

This book stinks.

BECAUSE IT'S THE WORST HALLOWEEN BOOK IN THE WHOLE ENTIRE WORLD!!!

And you're still here.

Is it because you are...

Curious?

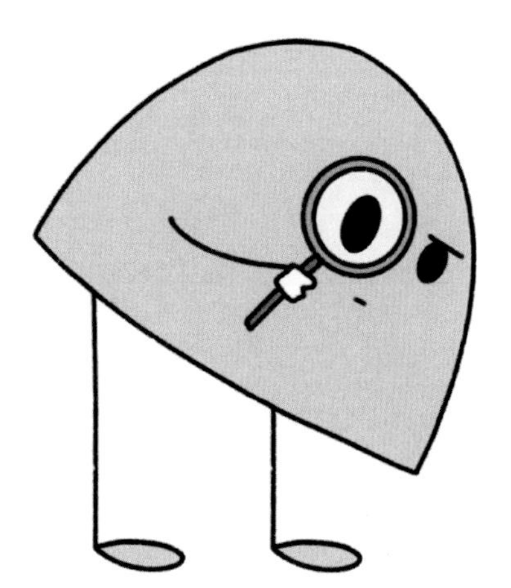

LIKE A CAT?!?

Ahhhhhhh!

Reason #1: there is a giant creepy
cat in this book.

Which I’m sure we’ll see again…

Reason #2: there is no trick-or-treating in this book.

I don't really like trick-or-treating, but I LOOOOOOOVE candy!!!

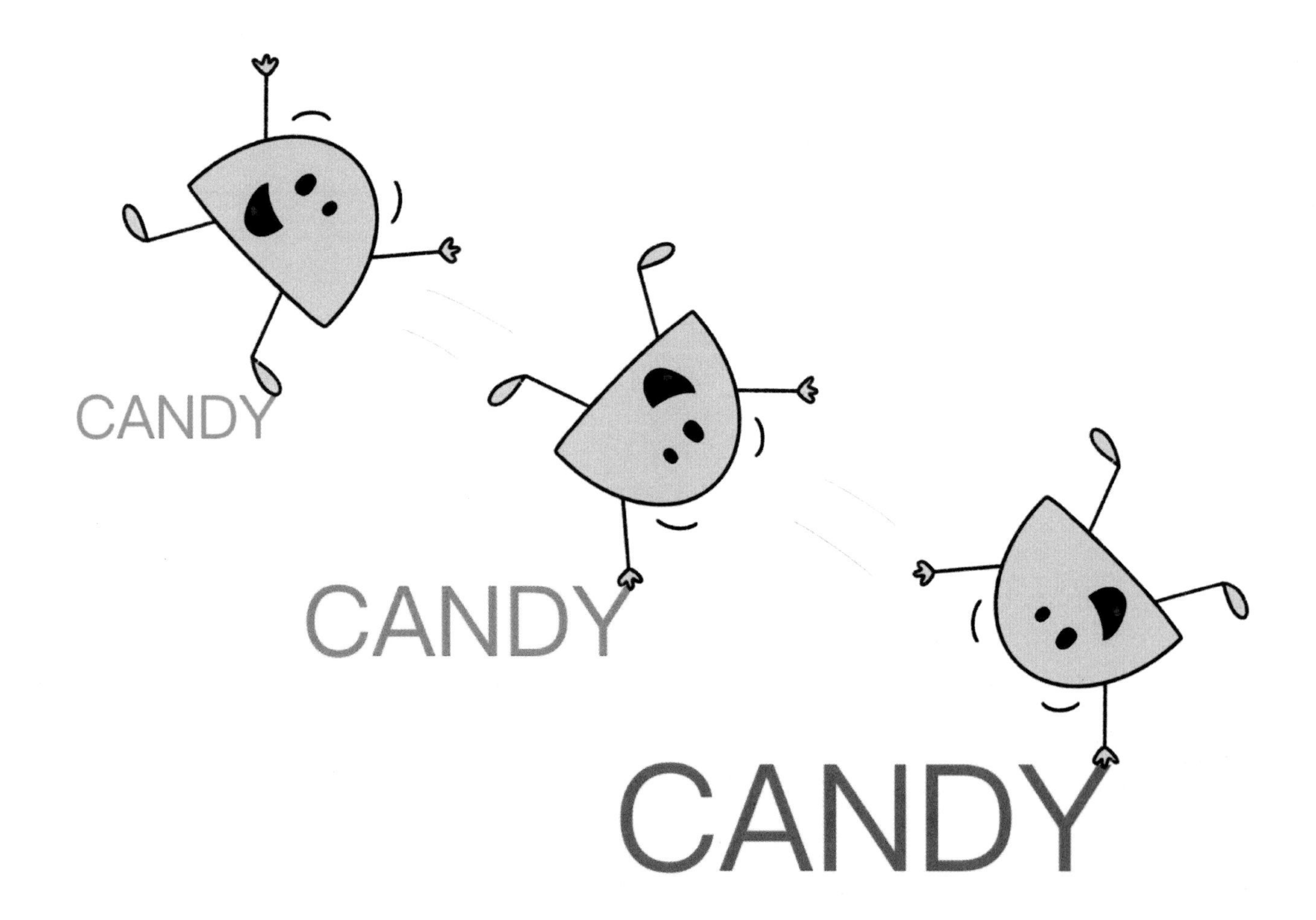

Reason #3: now I want some candy!

KNOCK

KNOCK

I'm not in a room and there's no door...

KNOCK

KNOCK

Come in?

Who are you?

I'm
Jerry Pumpkins!!!

Reason #4: I'm talking to a pumpkin...named Jerry.

Let's go
trick-or-treating!!!

No.

Why not?!?

Because I already told everyone there is no trick–or–treating in this book!

Okay! That means there'll be more candy for me...

Fine! I’m coming!

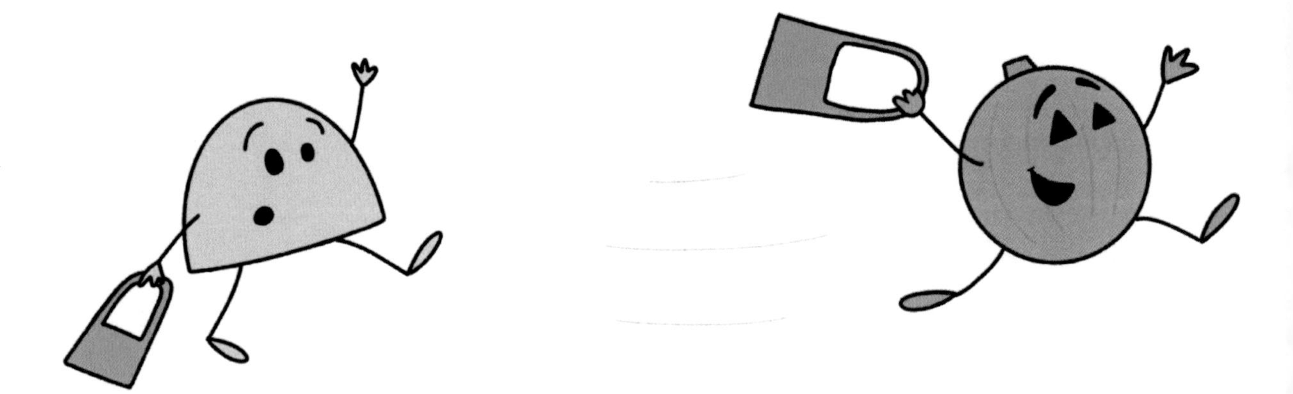

But where are we
going??

There!

Reason #5: Jerry Pumpkins wants to go trick-or-treating at a super scary castle AND we don't even have costumes!

But I want candy...

TRICK-OR-TREAT!

TRICK!

AHHHHHHHH!!!

AHHHHHHHHH!!!

The **TRICK** to making my delicious stew is one **rock** and one **pumpkin**!

Reason #6: I am now mad
at Jerry Pumpkins.

What is that, Jerry?

THERE IS NO SUCH
THING AS A CAT WHI....

It's my cat whistle!

MEEEOOOOOW!

Reason #7: GIANT
CREEPY CAT IS BACK!!!

We're saved, but we still don't have any candy.

There's something I need to tell you guys...

I'm really a giant magic

CANDY cat!

HAPPY HALLOWEEN!

Made in the USA
Coppell, TX
28 August 2021